This book belongs to:

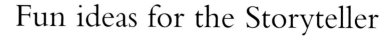

Fun ideas for the Storyteller

I Like Me invites children to think independently and feel good about themselves and others. Children will soon get the hang of the catchy repetitive phrasing and want to add their own ideas. It's an ideal starting point for discussion – and celebration!

Read on to find out how to get the most fun out of this story.

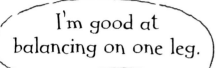

I'm good at balancing on one leg.

I like my brown hair and the pictures I draw.

Making it fun

This rhythmical text is just right for reading aloud. Children will want to stop and talk about the text and pictures as you read. Encourage them to act out their own 'I likes', and to add to the list of things they like about themselves and enjoy doing. Join in, too!

I like the clothes I wear.

Sharing the reading

The lively repetitious text and the bold, colourful pictures give clues to help children predict what comes next. Point to the 'I likes' and let your child say them. He will enjoy participating and will begin to recognize the written words. Sharing the book in this way will make your child feel that he is becoming a reader.

I like the friends I make.

Talking about the story

This book provides the perfect opportunity to talk about people – their differences, similarities, feelings and, of course, likes and dislikes. Let your child lead the talking, then gently bring up ideas yourself. There are lots of positive images to look at and share!

Reading the pictures

The pictures invite comparisons and comments. Images that reflect your child's own experiences can help him make sense of the world. Similarly, seeing something that is not familiar, and asking questions, helps him to learn and understand. Encourage your child to point to things that he notices and to talk freely about them.

Enjoy the book and share your child's pleasure at meeting so many children!

I can run fast, too.

Wendy Cooling

Wendy Cooling
Reading Consultant

For Connor, LA
For Chica, Boussó, Giovanni, Francesco, Anna,
Alice, Sofia, Pietro, Stefano, AG

Dorling  Kindersley

LONDON, NEW YORK, SYDNEY, DELHI, PARIS,
MUNICH and JOHANNESBURG

First published in Great Britain in 2001
by Dorling Kindersley Limited,
9 Henrietta Street, London WC2E 8PS

2 4 6 8 10 9 7 5 3 1

Text copyright © 2001 Laurence Anholt
Illustrations copyright © 2001 Adriano Gon

A CIP catalogue record for this book is available from the British Library.
ISBN 0-7513-7238-2

Colour reproduction by Dot Gradations, UK
Printed by Wing King Tong in China

Acknowledgements:
Reading Consultant: Wendy Cooling **Series Educational Advisor:** Lianna Hodson
Photographer: Steve Gorton **Models:** Ryan Heaton, Cherise Stephenson, Luke and Ivana Silva

see our complete
catalogue at
www.dk.com

I Like Me

Laurence Anholt

illustrated by Adriano Gon

A Dorling Kindersley Book

I like the way I look.
I like the clothes I wear.

I like the way
I roll my tongue.

I like
the way
my hair
sticks up
in the
morning.

I like my freckles.

I like the
gaps between
my teeth.

I like my body. My body belongs to me.
I eat good things and exercise to make
myself strong. Because I like me.

I don't look like people in magazines or on TV.
I look like myself and I like me.

I like me because I think for myself.
I don't follow the crowd.
I can stand up tall and hold
my head up high.

I like my
white skin.

I like my
brown skin.

I take care of myself because I like me.

I brush my teeth.

Because it makes me feel good and I like me.

I like the pictures I paint.

I like the things I make.

I like the castles I build.

I like the dreams I dream.

When I like me I can do
ANYTHING AT ALL.

Yes, I like me

and
I like
you
too.!

Activities to Enjoy

I f you've enjoyed this story, you might like to try some of these simple, fun activities with your child.

I like skipping.

Act it out

Build self-confidence and awareness of others by taking turns to show each other the things you're good at: running fast, pulling funny faces, writing your name, counting to ten, telling stories . . . Talk about the things you're not so good at, too. Perhaps teach each other how to do something you do well.

I like counting.

We like playing games

Mirror faces

Look in the mirror and talk about what you see. This will prompt your child to observe details like eye colour, freckles, and hair style. Try making faces to match different feelings: happy, sad, surprised, angry. Talk about what makes your child happy, or angry, or sad. What does he do when he feels this way?

If you're happy and you know it

Playing games that excercise different parts of your body are great for building physical awareness and self-esteem. Here are some you might know: "Simon Says"; "One Finger, One Thumb"; "Red Light, Green Light"; "If You're Happy".

If You're Happy

If you're happy and you know it, clap your hands.
If you're happy and you know it, clap your hands.
If you're happy and you know it, and you really want to show it,
If you're happy and you know it, clap your hands.

Verse 2
Stamp your feet

Verse 3
Nod your head

Verse 4
Turn around

Verse 4
Shout "We are!"
(Traditional)

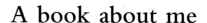

A book about me

Encourage your child to draw pictures of his achievements, his friends, and his family. Offer to write captions: "I like my black hair"; "I like my smile"; "I'm good at running". Bind the pictures together to make your own "I Like Me" book that your child can keep on his bookshelf.

Other Share-a-Story books to enjoy:

Clara and Buster Go Moondancing
   by Dyan Sheldon, illustrated by Caroline Anstey

Mama Tiger, Baba Tiger
   by Juli Mahr, illustrated by Graham Percy

Where's Bitesize?
   by Ian Whybrow, illustrated by Penny Dann

Not Now, Mrs. Wolf!
   by Shen Roddie,
   illustrated by Selina Young

Are You Spring?
   by Caroline Pitcher,
   illustrated by Cliff Wright

The Caterpillar That Roared
   by Michael Lawrence,
   illustrated by Alison Bartlett

Nigel's Numberless World
   by Lucy Coats, illustrated by Neal Layton